For Kite who sings in the night.

Cover and Graphic Design by Chanda Rule

How Butterfly Got her BEAUTIFUL wings

A STORY BY
CHANDA RULE

Long, long ago
when women were giants,
and treetops were chapels, and oceans were tame,
when Twitters and Tweets were sweet birdsongs
and Text had yet to be named...

It was Butterfly who sent The Message
and Butterfly who spread The Word.
BUTTERFLY
who kept the story
from the profound to the absurd.

Now, this job fit her quite well
because of her bright and solid color.
And of course,
HER PIERCING CRY
that could reach the ear like none other.

AIEEEEEEYAHAY!
AIEEEEEEYAHAH!
AIEEEEEEYAHOH!

SHE SANG,
WITH GLEEFUL SPINS AND GRACEFUL LEAPS
SHE DANCED AS HER CLEAR VOICE RANG.

All those who were near perked up with a cheer
when they heard her
MELODIC CRY.
For without doubt, The News was about
and Butterfly soon would come by.

Before **Mama Lion**
came strutting by proud
and bold with her new pride
Butterfly cried
"Bring gifts! Bring flowers!"
to animals far and wide.

AND BEFORE THE SCENT OF STORMS
AND SIGHT OF SKIES THAT TUMBLED 'ROUND,
BUTTERFLY WARNED THAT HEAVEN WOULD WATER THE EARTH
BEFORE SUN DROPPED DOWN.

AND WHEN CROCODILE WAS LOVESICK,
FEELING UNDERNEATH THE BLUES,
YES, BUTTERFLY WAS THE FIRST TO SPREAD THAT SAD AND WOEFUL NEWS.

AIEEEEEEYAHAY!
AIEEEEEEYAHAH!
AIEEEEEEYAHOH!

SHE WAILED.
WITH A MOURNFUL LILT
AND A SIGH-FILLED TILT
SHE SWOONED ON THE WINDS
AS SHE SAILED.

But as seasons turned and suns went by
with moons and years to follow,
Butterfly craved more excitement
because she thought her stories were hollow
and empty of words that stirred
or news that brought some titillation.
So Butterfly added more spice,
plus a dollop of imagination.

WITH AN ADDED TWIST, AN EXTRA TURN
AND A BIT OF HULLABALLOO,
BUTTERFLY'S EVERYDAY MESSAGES
GREW ASTOUNDING AND ANEW.

AIEEEEEEYAHAY!
AIEEEEEEYAHAH!
AIEEEEEEYAHOH!
SHE TITTERED.
WITH SWEEPING SPINS AND FLAMBOYANT FLIPS,
SHE GIGGLED AS SHE FLITTERED.

Next time Grandma Bear awoke
from her long and peaceful slumberings
with a growling yawn, a joyful roar
and a belly full of rumblings,

Butterfly cried,
"Oh! Bear's awake!
Her belly rumble is real.
Take care, take cover and watch out
or you'll be her very first meal!"

Now **GRANDMA BEAR** WAS CONCERNED
AND PEEVED BY THIS FALSE, UNKIND ACCUSATION.
ESPECIALLY SINCE ALL SHE WANTED TO EAT
WERE NUTS AND SPRING'S VEGETATION.

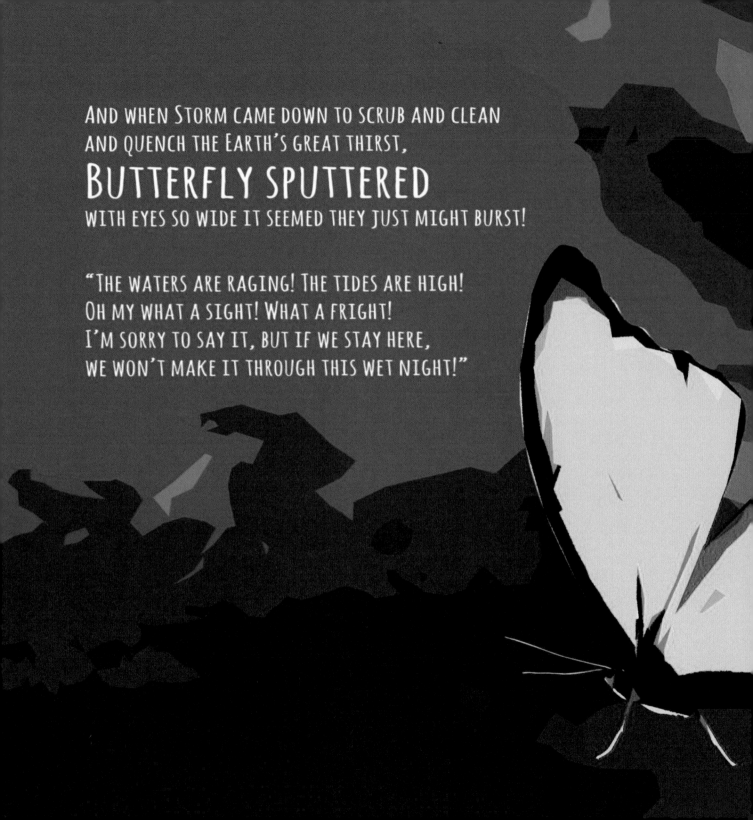

And when Storm came down to scrub and clean
and quench the Earth's great thirst,
BUTTERFLY SPUTTERED
with eyes so wide it seemed they just might burst!

"The waters are raging! The tides are high!
Oh my what a sight! What a fright!
I'm sorry to say it, but if we stay here,
we won't make it through this wet night!"

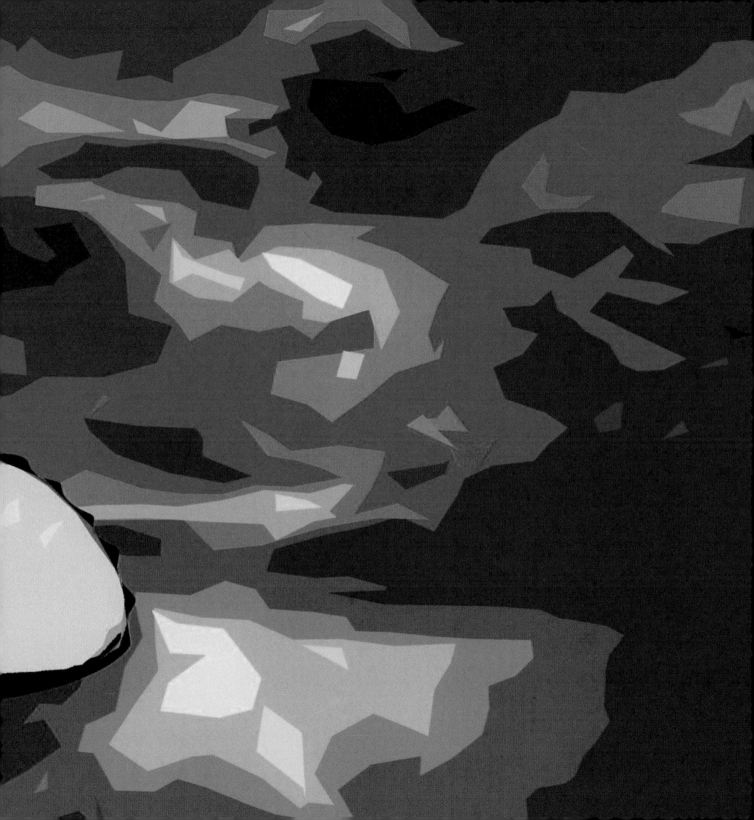

AND THROUGH ALL OF THE HOOPLAH OF RUNNING AND PACKING
AND MOURNING THE LANDS THEY WERE LEAVING,
BUTTERFLY WATCHED
FROM THE TREETOPS,
LAUGHING
SO HARD SHE WAS
HEAVING!

No one said a thing

about Butterfly's change or the new sensation of The Word,
but everyone, even the Rocks and the Bush
whispered the news that they heard.

THEN ONE MORNING BEFORE THE TREES
WERE OVERCOME WITH DAWN'S DEW
BUTTERFLY TOLD A BIG OL' STORY THAT WAS

DOWNRIGHT UNTRUE.

On an early flutter
she saw Blackbird playing in a hidden pool.
Beside her was Baby Giant just a'splashing and keeping cool.

But according to Butterfly,
Bird flew away with a wailing baby after dusk.
And what happened next is not hard to predict
as such news caused quite a big fuss.

The Giants
MOANED AND STOMPED AND WAILED,
CAUSING TREMORS FAR AND WIDE.
THE BIRDS WERE RILED AND SO UPSET
THEY HICCUPPED AS THEY CRIED.

NOT TO MENTION THAT THROUGHOUT THE VILLAGE
QUITE MANY WERE SCATTERED ABOUT.
DUE TO CONFUSION FROM SUCH AN EXTREME
WEATHER WARNING, NO DOUBT.

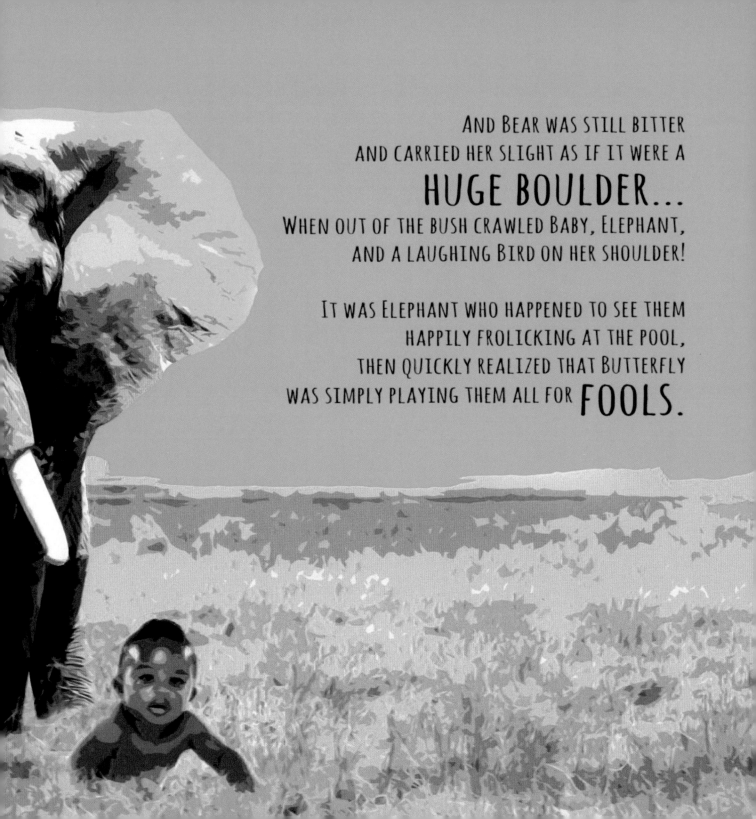

And Bear was still bitter
and carried her slight as if it were a
HUGE BOULDER...
When out of the bush crawled Baby, Elephant,
and a laughing Bird on her shoulder!

It was Elephant who happened to see them
happily frolicking at the pool,
then quickly realized that Butterfly
was simply playing them all for FOOLS.

So Elephant called out far and wide with a sound like

TRUMPETS AND THUNDER

For everyone to come hither, from the treetops to down under.

With a gentle voice like the softest rain she said to Butterfly,
"Your news and words have grown quite loose,
and they're littered with gossip and lies.

WORDS HOLD A MAGIC

and you are the keeper. How dare you abuse such a gift!
I believe a change is in order... Oh yes, it's time for a shift!"

WITH A SHAKE OF HER HIPS,
A POWER UNKNOWN, A SPIN, A BREATH AND A SIGH,
ELEPHANT USED HER OWN MAGIC TO SHUSH MS. BUTTERFLY.

THE WORDS SHE'D MISUSED WERE QUICKLY INFUSED
IN PATTERNS ACROSS HER BRIGHT WINGS.
SO INSTEAD OF A LOUD AND MELODIOUS CRY
A WHISPER IS ALL SHE COULD SING.

BUTTERFLY HOVERED WITH A QUIET SIGH
KNOWING WHAT SHE'D DONE WAS WRONG.
BUT DECIDED TO KEEP ON SPREADING THE WORD
WITH A NEW AND SILENT SONG.

WITH HER **BEAUTIFUL WINGS**
TELLING TALES OF THEIR OWN
SHE FLEW FROM FLOWER TO FLOWER,

AND WHISPERED TO ALL WHO WOULD LISTEN
TO ONLY USE WORDS THAT
EMPOWER.

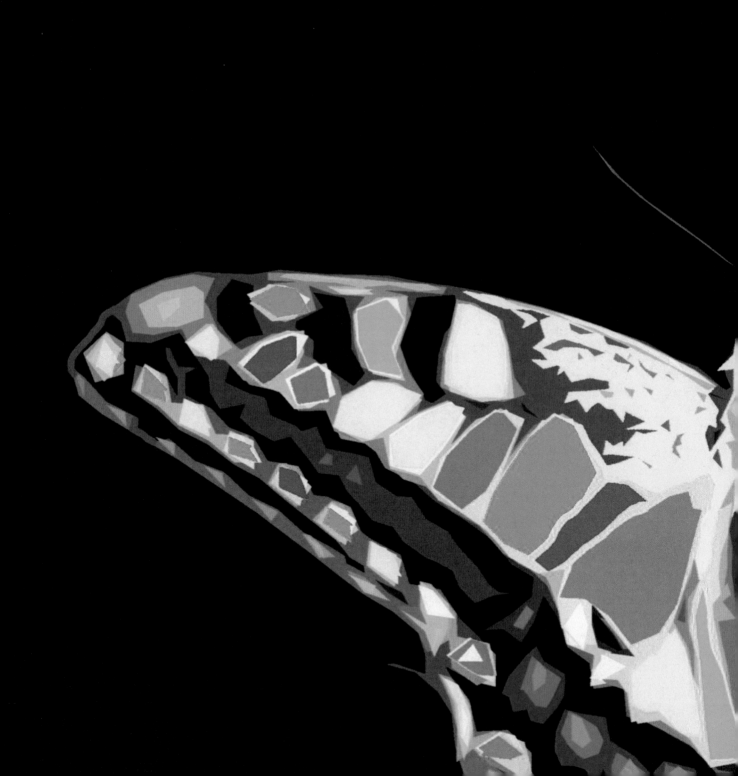

The End

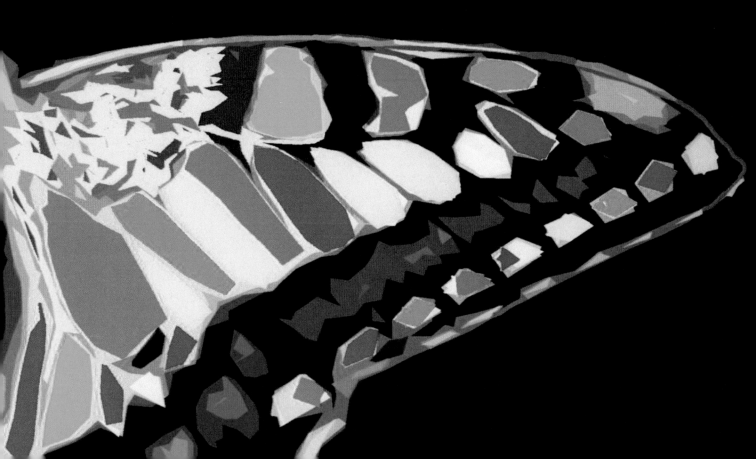

Glossary

Absurd: Something that is really silly
Accusation: Saying that someone did something wrong
Astounding: Surprising
Dollop: A little bit
Empower: To support and/or strengthen
Flamboyant: Flashy or over-done
Frolicking: To play and have fun
Gleeful: To be very happy
Hither: To go towards a place
Hollow: When something is empty; A person can also feel empty of emotion
Hooplah: Lots of chaos
Hullabaloo: A lot of fuss and confusion
Infused: To fill up
Lilt: A sing-song way of talking

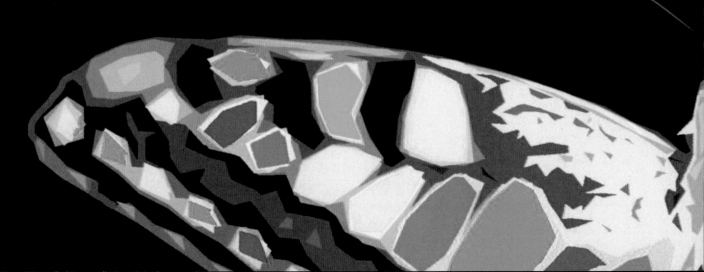

Melodic: Something that holds a melody or tune
Melodious: Having a really nice melody
Mournful: A very sad feeling
Piercing: Very loud and high-pitched
Pride: A group of lions that live and hunt together
Profound: Wise and full of meaning
Quench: To drink enough so you are not thirsty
Riled: Very upset
Sputter: To stutter from excitement
Swoon: To feel week or unsteady because of an emotion
Tame: Calm
Titillation: Excitement
Tremor: A vibration; Tremors are often felt before earthquakes
Woeful: An awful feeling

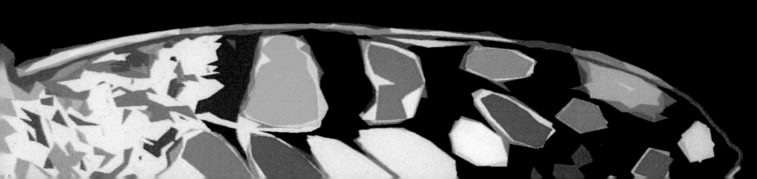

A FEW CONVERSATION STARTERS FOR YOUR FAMILIES & COMMUNITIES!

WHAT DOES IT MEAN TO EMPOWER?

WHY DO YOUR WORDS MATTER?

WHY DO YOU THINK BUTTERFLY SANG
TO SPREAD THE NEWS?

HOW DO YOU IMAGINE BUTTERFLY EMPOWERING
OTHERS AFTER SHE CHANGED?

WHAT ARE SOME WAYS YOU CAN USE WORDS, STORIES
AND EXPERIENCES TO EMPOWER OTHERS?

CHANDA RULE HAS BEEN WEAVING STORIES THROUGH SONG, HUMMING MELODIES, AND BENDING WORDS SINCE HER CHILDHOOD. SHE LOVES TO USE MUSIC AND STORY FOR COMMUNITY-BUILDING AND COMMUNAL HEALING. CHANDA LIVES IN VIENNA WITH HER HUSBAND, HER ROCK STAR SON AND HIS HOST OF INSTRUMENTS AND PLAYMOBIL PEOPLE. SHE IS CURRENTLY DREAMING OF WARM BREAD BAKING, HUMMING NEW TUNES, AND REFRAMING CHILDHOOD STORIES.

Made in the USA
Middletown, DE
20 May 2021

40144628R00029